FAT SANTA

Margery Cuyler
Pictures by Marsha Winborn

Henry Holt and Company · *New York*

For Juliana McIntyre, also a writer—M.C.

Library of Congress Cataloging in Publication Data
Cuyler, Margery.
Fat Santa.
Summary: When Santa becomes stuck in Molly's chimney,
she helps deliver the rest of his gifts.
[1. Santa Claus—Fiction.   2. Christmas—Fiction]
I. Winborn, Marsha, ill.   II. Title.
PZ7.C99Fat   1987   [E]   86-31962
ISBN: 0-8050-0423-8 (hardcover)
3   5   7   9   10   8   6   4   2
ISBN: 0-8050-1167-6 (paperback)
1   3   5   7   9   10   8   6   4   2

First published in hardcover in 1987
by Henry Holt and Company, Inc.
First Owlet edition 1989

Printed in the United States of America

More than anything in the world, Molly wanted to meet Santa Claus. Every Christmas Eve, after her parents had gone to bed, she'd creep downstairs, wrap a blanket around her shoulders, snuggle into an easy chair, and wait for Santa. The clock would chime eleven, then twelve, then one o'clock. She'd try to keep her eyes open, but by two o'clock, she would be asleep. The next morning, she'd wake up and find extra presents piled under the tree. And once again, Molly would have missed Santa.

But this Christmas, Molly was determined to see him. After she settled into the chair, she plugged in her earphones and listened to Christmas carols on her tape deck. The music helped her stay awake for awhile, but at two o'clock, her head nodded, her eyes grew heavy, and she started breathing deeply. The clock struck three. Then four. But at four-thirty, Molly heard a great thud. Her eyes popped open.

"I shouldn't have eaten that big bowl of plum pudding,"
said a growly voice. "The elves *told* me this would happen!"
Great clouds of soot were billowing out of the fireplace.
"I can't move up and I can't move down. What am I

going to do?" The voice was coming from the chimney.

Molly crept closer to have a look. As the soot cleared,
two shiny black boots dangled in front of her eyes.

"Santa?" she asked. "Is that really you?"

The feet shook.

"Of course it's me!" answered the growly voice. "Who else would be stuck in a chimney on Christmas Eve?"

Molly's hand flew to her mouth.

"I'll go wake my parents," she said. "They'll know what to do!"

"Don't waste your time!" said Santa. "Grown-ups can't see me. And children shouldn't either. But as long as you're here, maybe you can help me."

Molly sat down to think. Suddenly, she had an idea. She ran to her father's workshop and got a long rope. Then she ran back to the living room and tied one end around Santa's boots. She tied the other end to the door.

"When I say 'Merry Christmas,'" she told Santa, "suck in your breath."

"What are you going to do?" asked Santa.

"You'll see," said Molly.

"Merry Christmas!" she shouted. She waited until Santa took a deep breath. Then she slammed the door shut. Luckily, no one upstairs woke up. She looked at the fireplace. Santa's socks and boots were lying in the ashes.

"My toes are cold!" yelled Santa. "And I'm still stuck. It's getting late, and I need to get to the Perkins's house. I'll never deliver their presents at this rate."

"Don't worry," said Molly. "I know something else we can try."

She raced to the broom closet and grabbed a feather duster. Then she raced back to the fireplace and started tickling Santa's feet.

"Ho, ho, ho," bellowed Santa. "Ho, ho, ho, ha, ha, ha!"

More soot fell down the chimney and Santa's feet twitched and trembled. But he didn't budge.

"Rats!" said Molly. She sucked on the end of her finger. "I have another idea!" she cried.

She dashed to the kitchen and got some black pepper. Then she dashed back to the living room and started tossing it up the fireplace.

"Breathe deeply," she said.

She heard some wheezing and sputtering, then "ah-ah-ah-ah-CHOO!" More clouds of soot came pouring out of the fireplace, and there was a crashy thump. Molly gasped as she saw Santa struggling to climb out of the ashes. He was as

round as a snowball and his skin was as shiny as satin.

Santa stumbled onto the rug.

"Thanks," he said. "Now I need help with my boots. Mercy, I've got to hurry."

The clock was striking five o'clock. Molly bent over and stuffed Santa's pink feet into his socks and boots. Then she watched as Santa reached into his sack and pulled out some presents. "Please put these under the tree while I fill the stockings," he said.

When they finished working, Santa waddled to the fire-place. Just as he was about to climb up the chimney, he stopped. "Mercy, I could get stuck again, and the Perkins's chimney is much smaller."

He tugged several times on his beard. "Do you have any other suggestions?" he asked Molly.

But Molly had run out of ideas.

Suddenly, Santa clapped his hands. "I've got it!" he said. "*You* can deliver the Perkins's presents!"

"Me?" asked Molly.

"It's easy," said Santa. "My reindeer know where to go. All you have to do is climb up the chimney and get into my sleigh."

Molly looked up the chimney. It was black and dirty. She looked out the window. Outside was lonely and cold.

"I know you can do it!" said Santa. "Get your boots on!"

He took off his warm red coat and hat and put them on Molly. He pushed her toward the fireplace. "Scoot!" he said.

Before Molly could make up her mind, Santa lifted her into the chimney. It was dark, but she could feel the footholds. She carefully climbed to the top.

She gasped when she stepped out on the roof. Santa's eight reindeer glowed like golden shadows in the moonlight. They shuffled and snorted as she got into the sleigh. She jerked the reins. The reindeer leaped into the early morning air and glided across the sky, leaving a trail of silver behind them. They landed gently on the Perkins's roof.

Molly grabbed the sack of presents and lifted herself over the edge of the chimney. She climbed down very slowly and crawled into the Perkins's living room.

As quick as a spider, she arranged the presents around the tree and stuffed the stockings. Then she clambered back up the chimney and climbed into the sleigh.

A few lights were beginning to go on in some houses, and Molly knew she had to hurry. She looked down and saw Santa in the distance, waving at her from her front yard.

The reindeer flew to Molly's house and swirled down to the ground as softly as snowflakes.

Santa hugged her tightly. Then he carried her inside. Her eyelids were beginning to feel heavy. He took back his coat and hat and gently dropped her into her favorite chair.

"Merry Christmas," he whispered. "Happy New Year," he added as he tiptoed away.

Molly didn't wake up until her parents came downstairs an hour later.

"Did you see Santa this year?" her mother asked.

Molly rubbed her eyes sleepily. "I think I dreamed about him," she said.

But while she was opening her presents, she found a box wrapped in shiny paper. She tore off the paper and lifted out a gold star that shimmered as brightly as a lighted candle.

"I'll put it on top of the tree," said Molly. "I wonder who it's from?"

Then she read the note that came with it. It said:

Thanks for all your help. See you next year.
Love, Santa